DATE DUE

JAN 1 0 2012		
FEB 2 0 2012		
MAR 1 6 2012		
MAY 2 5 2012		
JUN 3 0 2012		
NOV 2 1 2012		
DEC 1 1 2012		
JAN 1 1 2013		

Demco, Inc. 38-293

NICK JR.

DORA the EXPLORER

E
V3l3

Happy Mother's Day, Mami!

by Leslie Valdes
illustrated by the Jason Fruchter

Simon Spotlight/Nick Jr.

New York   London   Toronto   Sydney   Singapore

Based on the TV series *Dora the Explorer*® as seen on Nick Jr.®

SIMON SPOTLIGHT
An imprint of Simon & Schuster Children's Publishing Division
1230 Avenue of the Americas, New York, New York 10020
Copyright © 2003 Viacom International Inc. All rights reserved.
NICKELODEON, NICK JR., *Dora the Explorer*, and all related titles, logos,
and characters are trademarks of Viacom International Inc.
All rights reserved, including the right of reproduction in whole or in part in any form.
SIMON SPOTLIGHT and colophon are registered trademarks of Simon & Schuster.
Manufactured in the United States of America
First Edition
2 4 6 8 10 9 7 5 3 1
ISBN 0-689-85233-9

Today is Mother's Day! *¡El Día de las Madres!* I'm making a special cake for my *mami*. Will you help me make the cake? Great!

First we need to find the recipe card for the banana-nut-chocolate cake. Do you see the recipe card that has bananas, nuts, and chocolate?

Here's the recipe card! But where can we find bananas, nuts, and chocolate? Let's ask the Map. Say, "Map!"

Map says we have to go to the Banana Grove, then through the Nutty Forest, and finally to the Chocolate Tree! Then we'll have all the ingredients to make my *mami's* cake.

Look! It's my friend Boots the monkey!
Boots drew a picture for his mommy for Mother's Day.

Come on, let's go to the Banana Grove! Do you see the grove?

We made it to the Banana Grove. We need three bananas for the cake. The bananas need to be yellow—that means they're ripe! Do you see three yellow bananas?

Good counting!

Hey, look, it's our friend Benny the bull. Hi, Benny! He gave a cowbell to his grandma for Mother's Day. What a nice gift!

¡*Vámonos!* Let's go to the Nutty Forest. We still have to get the other ingredients. Bye, Benny!

Here we are at the Nutty Forest. And there's our friend Tico the squirrel. He's giving his mommy a bracelet made of nuts for Mother's Day. It's so pretty.

We need to collect six nuts. Let's count them in Spanish: *uno, dos, tres, cuatro, cinco, seis!*

You did it! Good counting!

Hey, look, it's our friend Isa the iguana. Hi, Isa!
Isa is gathering flowers to give to her mommy for
Mother's Day.

Oh, no! Look! There's Swiper the fox. That sneaky fox is trying to swipe Isa's flowers. Say, "Swiper, no swiping!"

You did it! You saved Isa's flowers! Now we have to go to the Chocolate Tree. Do you see the Chocolate Tree?

Come on, let's go get the last ingredient for my *mami's* special cake!

We made it to the Chocolate Tree! It only has one piece of chocolate left, and it's way up high. Can you help us reach it? Put your hands in the air and reach really high!

Yay! You reached the chocolate! Now we have all the ingredients. Let's go home and make the cake.

This is my daddy, *mi papi*. He's going to help us make the cake. First we put all the ingredients into a bowl and mix them up. *Bate, bate, bate!* Mix, mix, mix!

After we mix all the ingredients *Papi* will put the cake in the oven to bake. The cake will be ready soon. Thanks for helping!

It's time to give my *mami* the special cake!

Mami says it's delicious—*¡delicioso!*

Happy Mother's Day, *Mami!*